This edition first published 2002 by Brown Watson
Reprindted 2003
The Old Mill, 76 Fleckney Road
Kibworth Beauchamp, Leics LE8 0HG

ISBN: 0-7097-1502-1

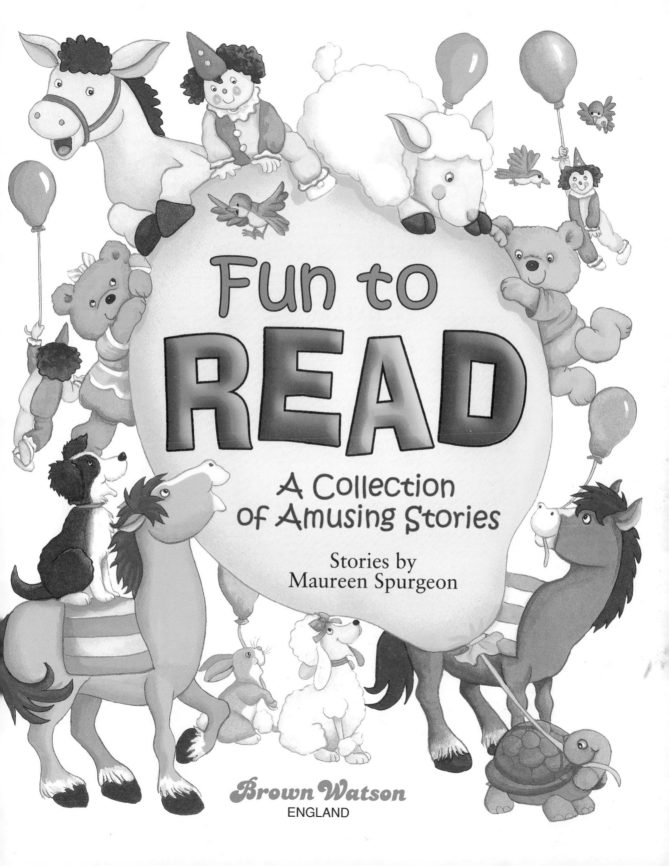

Fun to READ

A Collection of Amusing Stories

Stories by
Maureen Spurgeon

Brown Watson
ENGLAND

CONTENTS

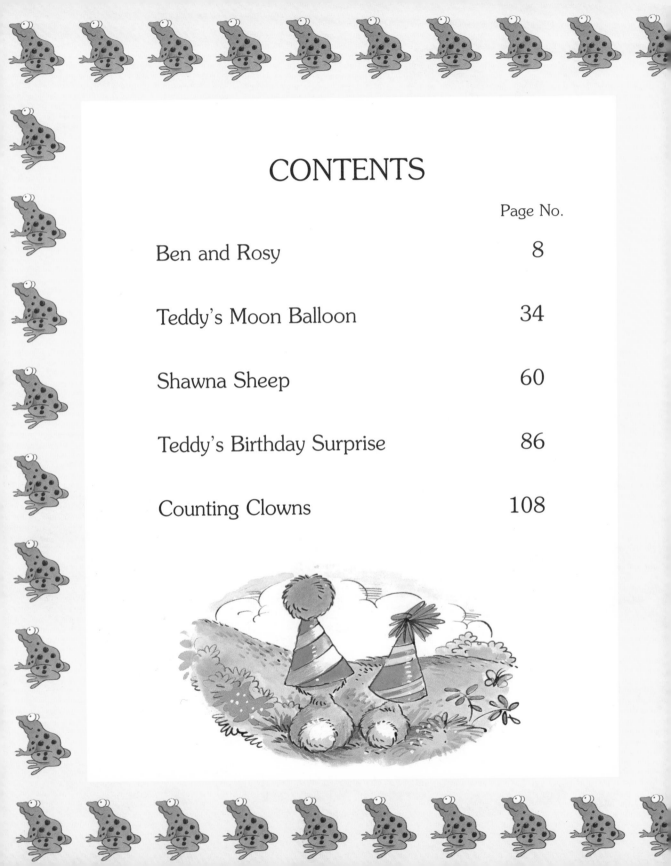

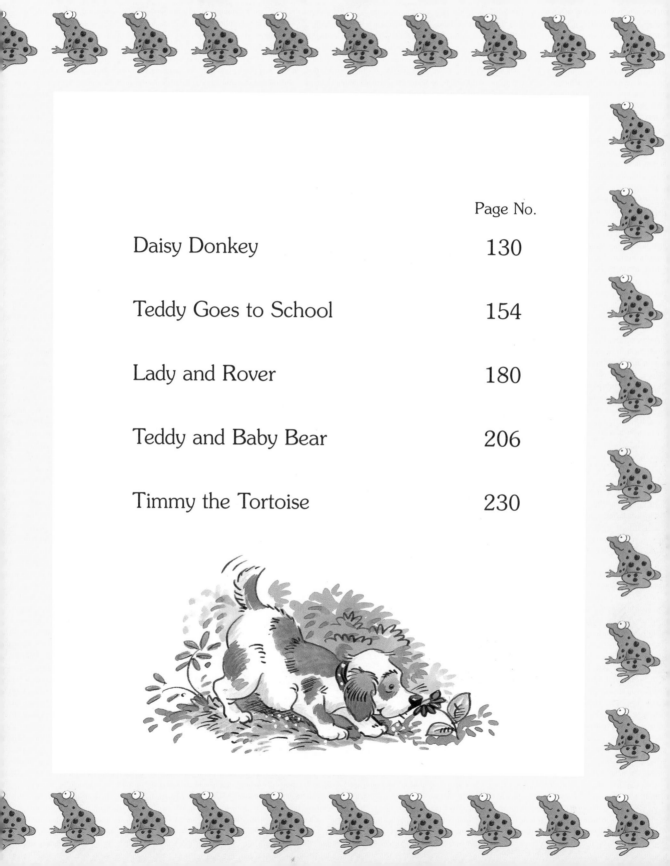

Ben and Rosy

Ben and Rosy were two big, strong horses. They had worked at Hill Farm for a long, long time. 'Your Grandad had Ben and Rosy when I was a boy,' Farmer West told his children, Jack and Susan. 'Hill Farm would not be quite the same without them!'

'But,' he went on, 'they are getting old and they are getting slow. I think it is time that we made some changes at Hill Farm!'
Jack and Susan looked at each other. What did their dad mean?

They soon found out! One morning there came a loud 'BEEP! BEEP!' and two big, black wheels and something shiny and red appeared! 'Dad has bought a tractor!' shouted Susan.

'And Mum is driving it!' added Jack. They stopped feeding the chickens and went to get a closer look. Mum and Dad looked very pleased. The tractor looked so bright and cheerful!

'Meet Toby the tractor!' Mum said. 'He can pull a plough, clear a ditch, tow a trailer, move heavy loads...'
'But Ben and Rosy do all that!' said Susan. 'What work will they do?'

'They can have a rest!' said Dad. 'The tractor can do their work in half the time!' That was true. With the tractor it was possible to plough a field, dig a ditch and put up a fence in one day!

And the tractor still looked bright and cheerful, not at all tired!
'Good old Toby the tractor!' said the farmer.
He even gave the tractor's front wheel a pat, just like he used to pat Ben and Rosy!

'It seems very strange for us not to be working on the farm,' Ben said to Rosy. 'I do not like it,' Rosy said to Ben. 'With no work for us to do, there is no need for the farmer to keep us here!'

'No need to talk like that!' said Ben. 'Toby
the tractor cannot do everything!'
But Rosy shook her big head sadly.
'It seems to me,' she said, 'there is nothing
that tractor cannot do!'

This time, Ben said nothing. He had a horrible feeling that Rosy might be right. How long would the farmer be able to let them stay if the tractor was doing their work?

Ben lifted his big head up to the sky.
'Let us go into our stable,' he said. 'It looks
like rain.' Rosy stamped her big hooves.
She tried not to look at Farmer West
working with the tractor again.

'That is all the planting done!' he called to his wife. 'Just in time before a spell of bad weather, too! And it's all thanks to our new tractor!' He just managed to lock up the shed as rain began to fall.

It rained all night long. Ben and Rosy heard it beating down on the roof of their stable. Early next day, the door opened and in came Jack and Susan in their rainhats and wellington boots.

'Hello, Ben and Rosy,' said Jack.
'Here are your oats and some hay,' said
Susan. But before Ben and Rosy had
begun to eat, there came a loud cry from
the yard outside.

'Come along, Toby!' cried Farmer West. 'We have work to do! The rain has washed away so much soil from Bottom Field that our new fence has started to fall down! It is sliding into the stream!'

Then came the sound of the tractor starting up. Jack and Susan left Ben and Rosy in the stable and ran to see what was happening. The rain had made the ground muddy and slippery.

But Toby the tractor looked as bright and as cheerful as ever! By the time Jack and Susan reached Bottom Field, he was already lifting the pieces of fence out of the stream!

Each piece was loaded carefully into the farm trailer. Then, Farmer West hooked the trailer to the back of the tractor. Everyone looked very pleased. Jack and Susan felt like cheering!

Then, Farmer West got back into the driving seat and started up the engine. Toby the tractor made a lot of noise as he tried to pull the heavy trailer. His wheels spun round in the muddy ground.

Toby tried to go forwards, but he could not move! The more his wheels spun round, the deeper he sank into the mud. 'Drat!' cried Farmer West. 'Now, what can we do?'

Just then there came the sound of plodding hooves from the old stables.
'Ben and Rosy!' cried Susan.
'Ben and Rosy!' cried Jack. 'They can pull the tractor out of the mud!'

Ben and Rosy were led to Bottom Field. Soon, their big strong hooves were plodding slowly across the soggy, muddy ground as they made their way towards Toby the tractor.

They could see that Toby was very pleased to see them! Farmer West worked quickly to fasten their harness firmly to the front of the tractor. 'Over to you, Ben and Rosy!' he said. 'Pull!'

Ben and Rosy pulled hard. In no time
at all, they had pulled the tractor, the
heavy trailer and all the pieces of
fencing out of the muddy ground and
onto dry land!

This time, Jack and Susan really did cheer! 'Good old Ben and Rosy! We still need them to work on our farm!' Toby winked his headlights to show that he quite agreed.

Teddy's Moon Balloon

One morning, Teddy Bear had just eaten his porridge, when – guess what he saw through the window? A big, yellow balloon! A big yellow balloon with a ticket tied to the string! Teddy watched it bouncing and bobbing along as the breeze lifted it up into the sky. There were lots of other balloons, too!

"There's a balloon race in the meadow today, Teddy," smiled Daddy Bear. "It's to raise money for the toys' hospital."

"Balloon race?" said Teddy. "What's that?" So Daddy explained.

"Every bear who buys a balloon writes their name on a ticket. When the balloons go up in the air, the bear whose name is on the balloon which goes the furthest, wins the race!"

Teddy wanted a big, yellow balloon like the one he had seen outside his window! By the time his turn came to put his name on a ticket, there was only one left. Teddy did like its round, smiley face!

It was such a lovely, big, smiley balloon that Teddy didn't want to let go of the string. Then a gust of wind tugged it out of his paw and away it went, up and up, higher and higher into the sky.

"When's the race over?" he asked. "When we know which balloon has travelled the furthest," said Mummy. "So if your balloon goes further than anyone else's, you win a prize!"

"But my balloon WILL come back," Teddy said anxiously. "Won't it?" "Maybe," said Daddy at last. "If you wish hard enough!" So, for the rest of the day, Teddy kept wishing and wishing.

Teddy just could not stop thinking about his big, yellow balloon with the smiley face. And as it grew dark, he stared up at the sky, hoping he might see it again.

"Bedtime, Teddy!" said Daddy Bear.

"Want to see something big and yellow, with a smiley face?"

"My balloon?" gasped Teddy.

"Not quite," said Daddy, smiling. "But you are nearly right!"

"It's the Man in the Moon!" Daddy went on. "Isn't he like your balloon?" Teddy smiled and nodded. And the more he looked at the Man in the Moon, the nearer his smiley face seemed to get...

Suddenly, Teddy sat up, his eyes big and round. "YOU'RE not the Man in the Moon!" he cried, staring at the smiling face. "You're my big, yellow balloon!"

The balloon smiled and bobbed about. Teddy reached out to grab the string – and the next minute, he was sailing through the window, with the balloon lifting him up and up into the night sky!

"This is fun!" Teddy laughed.
And so it was. Lots of balloons were doing their best to be in the race. But none of them could catch Teddy and his big, yellow, smiley balloon!

The closer they got to the Man in the Moon, the bigger his round, yellow face became! "The winner!" he declared, in his deep, rumbly sort of voice. "Teddy Bear has won the balloon race!"

The balloon lifted Teddy Bear a tiny bit higher,
then they floated down on a soft cloud.
The Man in the Moon's smile was so bright, it
was almost like daytime – except for the stars
twinkling!

"What's this?" asked Teddy, holding out his paw towards a shower of beautiful silver balls drifting down. "Is it rain?"

"No!" chuckled the cloud. "They are moonbeams! Look!"

The cloud gave a little puff and a silver moonbeam floated onto Teddy's paw. "That's for winning the balloon race!" said the cloud. "And for coming to see ME!" boomed the Man in the Moon.

Before Teddy could speak, there was a flash in the sky, then a rumble, strong enough to shake the cloud. "I knew there'd be a storm," puffed the cloud, "as soon as my edges turned black."

"Time for you to go, Teddy Bear!" said the Man in the Moon. "Will you come and see me again?"

"Ooh, yes!" said Teddy, putting the moon-beams in his pocket. "Thank you very much!"

The big, yellow balloon gave a little tug on its string, taking Teddy Bear up into the air once more. Thunder rolled and the lightning flashed – but Teddy didn't mind, not one bit!

Soon, Teddy was back in his bed, with the big, yellow balloon smiling at him and the Man in the Moon playing Hide-and-Seek behind the clouds. Teddy watched him for a long time before he fell asleep.

"Quite a storm we had last night, Teddy!" said
Mummy Bear next day. "My – my balloon!"
cried Teddy, looking at the end of his bed.
"My big yellow balloon!"

Daddy laughed. "You're going to get it back after all, Teddy! Your balloon went the furthest and you've won the balloon race! What a splendid prize you've got!"

Teddy's prize was a journey in a real balloon! Up into the sky he went, his friends cheering and waving. And how different it all looked in the daytime!

There was no sign of the Man in the Moon, but Teddy knew he would see him later, smiling through his window. And he still had his moon beam, blown by a friendly cloud!

Shawna the Sheep

Farmer Nancy was proud of her sheep. Their wool was the finest that anyone had ever seen. The sheep with the best wool was Shawna. 'My wool is so soft!' she kept saying. 'People only come to Farmer Nancy to buy wool because I am here!'

One day, Shawna saw a lady and a man looking at all the other sheep in the meadow. Farmer Nancy was there too. 'Shawna!' she cried. 'I was just coming to find you!'

'Meet Kate and Bill!' said Farmer Nancy.
'They are going to spin wool this year at the
summer fair!'
'And it is your wool we want to spin!' said
Bill. 'Such fine, soft wool!'

This made Shawna feel very proud! Off she went in a smart trailer with Farmer Nancy, looking very grand! The day was fine and warm and she felt rather hot. But that did not matter!

There was a crowd waiting to see Shawna at the fair! Farmer Nancy took some wisps of wool from her fleece and Bill spun them into a long thread on his spinning wheel.

'This wool will be made into a lovely, soft scarf!' Kate told the crowd. 'It is the finest, softest wool that anyone can buy!' After that, everyone wanted to pet Shawna and feel her wool.

Shawna soon felt very hot indeed! But she tried not to mind. 'You are quite a famous sheep, Shawna!' said Farmer Nancy. 'But I am sure you will be glad when shearing begins tomorrow!'

'What is shearing?' said Shawna. But Farmer Nancy did not hear. Shawna had to wait until she was back at the farm. She went to see the other sheep.

'What is shearing?' she asked them.

'It's when you feel cooler!' said one.
'And lighter!' said another.
'And smaller!' added a third sheep.
'Cooler?' bleated Shawna. 'Lighter? Smaller? But, what IS shearing?'

'Don't you know?' another sheep bleated
back. 'Shearing is when you lose your
thick, woolly coat!'
And off they went, bleating in delight at the
look of shock on Shawna's face.

'N-no!' she cried. 'Not my lovely, soft wool?' But it was true. Next day, the shearers were busy peeling away the wool from each sheep. How bare they all looked afterwards!

They skipped and jumped around, feeling so light and so cool in the warm sunshine! But Shawna's mouth was wide open in horror. She did not want to lose her soft, fine wool!

Off she ran, feeling so very hot! She was glad to rest in the shade of a big tree. But, as the sun rose higher, the shadow of the tree became shorter, until there was no shade at all!

Feeling even hotter, Shawna ran into the dairy, where butter and cheese were made. There were tiles on the walls and on the floor, smooth and cool. Shawna began to feel better.

Then, a strong hand pushed her from behind. 'Out you go, Shawna!' said the dairyman. 'Today is shearing day! Time to lose your woolly coat!' And he pushed her out of the door!

Off she ran again until she came to a stream. Shawna put her feet into the cool water. 'That is better!' she said. 'I was feeling SO hot!' Still the sun beat down on her woolly back.

Then Shawna had another shock. It was Sam, the sheep-dog! 'Woof! Woof!' he barked. 'So here you are, Shawna! Farmer Nancy says you must come and get sheared!'

'I WILL not lose my fine, soft wool!' bleated
Shawna. 'I will NOT!' And off she ran. But
Sam could run faster. He darted in front, so
that she could go no further. Then Shawna
had an idea.

There was a wire fence around the field. Shawna began to squeeze under it. Sam, the sheep-dog, could not follow her now! Suddenly, she felt a strong tug at her coat.

'Baa!' bleated Shawna. Had Sam taken hold of her wool in his strong teeth? She tried to pull free.

'Woof!' barked Sam. 'You have caught your coat on the wire, Shawna!'

Sam ran to fetch Farmer Nancy.
'Hold still, Shawna!' she said. 'I must
cut you free. Then you can come and
have your fleece sheared properly! You
silly sheep!'

By now, Shawna was too tired and much too hot to do anything! All the other sheep were skipping about and enjoying the sunshine without their thick woolly coats.

The shearer soon cut away Shawna's fine, soft wool! 'It's a shame about the big hole in your fleece,' he said. 'That is where you caught your wool on the wire fence!' Poor Shawna!

But, she had to admit, she did feel very nice and cool! Then, Bill spun lots of woolly thread on his spinning wheel, ready for Kate to weave into beautiful scarves and shawls!

Their work won first prize at the town craft fair! 'Fine, soft sheep's wool makes beautiful things,' said Kate. And Shawna, standing in her pen beside Farmer Nancy, quite agreed!

Teddy's Birthday Surprise

Teddy Bear woke up, blinking at the sun shining into his room. The birds sang and chattered noisily. Downstairs, Mummy and Daddy Bear laughed and talked together. But why did it feel such a special sort of day?

"My birthday!" he remembered, jumping out of bed.

He hoped he would have lots of birthday cards, and Mummy and Daddy always let him open his presents at breakfast-time.

"Happy Birthday, Teddy!" called Mummy Bear, cheerfully.

"Many happy returns!" smiled Daddy. Teddy said nothing. There was one card beside his plate, but no presents – not even from Uncle Sailor Bill. And he never forgot birthdays!

"Maybe Mummy and Daddy haven't enough money to spend on parties and birthdays," thought Teddy.

He opened the card and up popped a little bear, smiling and waving at him!

"That's your first birthday surprise," laughed Daddy Bear.

Teddy Bear did like the card! He took it out into the garden, opening and closing it again and again.

Teddy was about to go back indoors, when he
saw Teacher Bear carrying a basket and two
shopping bags. They looked very heavy.
"Do you need any help, Teacher Bear?" he
asked, politely.

"Er – no thank you, Teddy," she said quickly.
"I – I think I can manage." And off she went
down the road just as fast as she could.
Teddy Bear was very surprised all over again.

Next minute, the sparrows and robins flew down and began pecking at some sausage roll crumbs on the ground. Teddy knew that they must have fallen from Teacher Bear's basket.

"I wonder where Teacher Bear was taking those sausage rolls?" thought Teddy. He loved sausage rolls!
He was still wondering when he heard voices by the back gate.

It was Honey Bear and Tiny Bear!
"Hurry up, you two," said Honey's mummy,
"or we won't get it all finished in time!"
"Get WHAT finished in time?" Teddy wanted
to know.

But they just went past. Honey Bear's mummy was pushing her shopping trolley with a big box on top. By now, Teddy was sure something was going on, something he didn't know about.

Then he heard voices whispering his name!
"Is that you, Billy Bear?" he called out.
Sure enough, the cheeky face of Billy Bear
peeped out from behind a big tree.

"Oh – er, hello, Teddy," he said. "We were all just going somewhere, weren't we, Bella?" Bella was Billy's little sister.

"What have you got hidden behind your back?" asked Teddy.

"Me?" said Billy. "Nothing!"

He and Bella ran off just as fast as they could possibly go!

"Hey!" shouted Teddy, loud enough for Mummy and Daddy to hear. "Come back here! Where are you both going?"

"What's wrong?" asked Mummy.
"I just don't know!" sighed Teddy. And he told them all that had happened. "Billy and Bella wouldn't even say where they were going!" he finished.

"Why don't we go the same way?" Daddy Bear suggested. "We might find out, then." So, they went along the path. Suddenly, Teddy saw something through the trees...

It was a bunch of balloons, bobbing in the breeze, with streamers and paper lanterns! Then came the sound of a guitar and voices began to sing, "Happy Birthday to You!"

"Happy Birthday, dear Teddy! Happy
Birthday to you!" Teddy was so surprised, he
couldn't speak! All his friends were there,
even Uncle Sailor Bill!

"Mummy had your birthday cake when you saw us!" laughed Honey. "Teacher Bear made the sausage rolls, and Tiny and I brought the balloons!"

"And look at all your presents!" smiled Barry
Bear proudly.
"It's a birthday picnic with games to follow!"
said Mummy. "We will all have such fun!"

"What do you think, Teddy?"

"Well," said Teddy, "I've already had lots of surprises today, but THIS is the best birthday surprise of all!" And, so it was.

COUNTING CLOWNS

1 to 10

Join the Counting Clowns,
And, then –
You'll soon learn
To count to ten!

One to ten

1

One dog pushes
One ball! What fun!
And, how many clowns?
That's right! There's one!

One

2

Two birds! Two rabbits!

And two clowns, too!

One drummer, one bugler –

Count them! One, two!

Two

3

Three butterflies,

Three places for tea.

Count the clowns on the see-saw,

There's one, two, three!

Three

4

One, two, three clowns –
And, then – one more!
How many on the boat?
One, two, three, four!

Four

5

Five fieldmice

Glad to be alive!

Counting Clowns, one
and two,

Three, four, five!

Five

6

Six pails for jolly clowns
Practising their tricks.

Climbing high, there's one,
  two, three,

Four, five, six!

Six

7

Jumping on a trampoline,

Clowns think this is heaven!

There's one, two, three and four,

Five, six, seven!

Seven

8

Holding on to eight balloons,

Clowns in such a state!

There's one, there's two –

There's three and four,

Five, six, seven, eight!

Eight

9

Clowns now climbing up a tree,

And everything is fine!

There's one, there's two, three,
    and four –

Five, six, seven, eight, nine!

Nine

10

Clowns are altogether, now –

So, count them once again!

One, two, three, four, five, six,
    seven –

Eight, nine, ten!

Ten

Daisy Donkey

Daisy Donkey was not at all dainty. She was big and clumsy, with bald patches on her coat. She had been called Daisy by Ken, a man at the animal shelter. 'Daisy has been badly treated,' he told Farmer Green.

'Could your Tom and Katie look after her?'
'Please, Dad!' cried Tom.
'Please!' added Katie. 'Daisy really needs a good home!'
Farmer Green nodded. 'She can stay on our farm,' he said. 'You can look after her!'

Tom and Katie were very glad! Daisy loved being on the farm. She would wait by the gate for them to get home from school. Then she would bend her head for them to scratch her long ears.

But she jumped at the slightest sound! If one of the farm dogs barked, or the cockerel crowed, or if a noisy lorry went past, Daisy would bray in fright! 'Hee-Haw! HEE-HAW!'

'No need to be frightened,' said Katie. She stroked Daisy along her back.
'Daisy was frightened by something which made a loud noise,' said Ken. 'She cannot forget it.'

The days became longer. Katie and Tom found a rug, a bridle and a saddle for Daisy. They put on riding hats and took turns to ride the little donkey and lead her around the meadow.

'It is lucky that Daisy came to your farm,'
Ken said. 'Our shelter was too small for her
to stay for long.'
'Can't you make the animal shelter bigger?'
asked Katie.

'We cannot afford it!' said Ken. 'But
we are hoping to make some money at
the Town Show next Saturday! Will
you come and buy something from our
stall?'

'You know we will!' said Katie. 'But I do wish we could help some more!'
'So do I,' said Tom. They both began to think hard. Daisy wanted to help too, nuzzling them with her long nose.

'I know!' said Katie at last. 'Let's wear some big posters saying – PLEASE HELP THE ANIMAL SHELTER – and take Daisy to the show! She can carry a tin to collect the money!'

Tom and Katie worked hard, drawing and painting the posters. Then, two posters were threaded on string, so that one poster would be at the front and the other at the back.

Farmer Green hung a collecting tin carefully around Daisy's neck. 'Put on your riding hat, Tom,' he said. 'You can ride Daisy to the show with Katie leading her!'

Daisy felt pleased with herself, and very proud. All along the way to the show, people came up and stroked and patted her, wanting to know about the animal shelter.

They put money in the collecting tin, too!
'Hee-haw!' cried Daisy each time a coin
clattered into the tin. Katie held the leading
rein firmly. 'It is all right, Daisy,' said Tom.
'It is all right.'

Children were blowing up balloons and making them go pop! 'Hee-Haw!' brayed Daisy in fright. Then a drum sounded. 'Boom-BOOM!' 'HEE-HAW!' went Daisy, louder still.

A line of horses with bells and ribbons went past Daisy. CRACK! Their trainer cracked her whip on the ground. She was telling the horses to turn a corner. CRACK! CRACK!

'HEE-HAW!' Daisy had never brayed quite so loudly. 'HEE-HAW! HEE-HAW!' She began to trot and then to run and then to gallop! 'Stop, Daisy!' shouted Tom. 'Please, stop!'

'Hee-haw! HEE-HAW!' It seemed to Tom that lots of other donkeys were joining in! He held on to Daisy with all his might! He wanted to shut his eyes tight, hardly daring to look up.

'Stop, young man!' someone shouted. You can stop now!'

'Hurrah!' someone else shouted. 'It's the donkey from the animal shelter! The one we saw on the road!'

Tom felt a strong arm around his back.
A hand pulled gently at Daisy's bridle
and Ken's calm voice spoke into her
long ears. 'It's all right, Daisy. 'It's all
right!'

Tom looked up at last, not feeling at all happy. 'I am sorry, Ken,' he began. 'We wanted to raise some money for the animal shelter, but...'
'And so you have!' Ken told him.

He gave a grin and waved a handful of money at Tom. 'Look! First prize for winning the Donkey Derby! And people are still giving us money! You and Daisy have done us proud!'

And how Daisy enjoyed being stroked and patted and told what a clever donkey she was! 'We're proud of you, Daisy,' said Katie. 'Lucky for us that you came to live on our farm!'

Teddy Goes to School

It was a beautiful day and Billy and Bella Bear had been playing with Teddy in his back garden.

They had all splashed about in the paddling pool. They had played ball games and Hide-and-Seek. Now, they were happy to sit in the warm sunshine, nibbling biscuits, drinking squash and chatting to each other.

Suddenly, Billy said: "We won't be doing this tomorrow!"

"Or the next day!" added Bella,

"Or the day after!" Billy went on. "We'll be at school!"

"I'm going to school tomorrow!" cried Teddy.
"Mummy Bear's bought me a satchel and a lunch-box and a pencil-case, and…"
"Poor you!" said Bella.
"Never mind!" added Billy.

Teddy blinked. He had been with Mummy and Daddy Bear to see Teacher Bear's school. It seemed a very nice place to be.

"Why?" he asked at last. "What's wrong with school?"

"No sweets!" said Bella.

"You can't take any toys!" added Billy. "Or talk to your friends! And, as for school dinners..."

"YUK!" shuddered Bella. "They're really horrible!"

Just then, Billy and Bella's daddy came to take
them home, so Teddy couldn't ask any more
questions about school. He had really thought
he would like it. Now, he wasn't so sure.

Mummy saw how worried Teddy was.
"You'll love Teacher Bear's School," she said.
"Wait and see!" Teddy felt better then. Mummy
Bear never said anything that wasn't true.

Next morning, Mummy packed Teddy's lunch-box.

"No sweets, Teddy," she said. "Teacher Bear doesn't like them being brought to school."
Teddy pulled a face.

"Cheer up!" smiled Mummy. You can have an apple and some crisps, instead."
"Put that toy down, Teddy!" called Daddy Bear. "Then we'll be off on our way."

"No sweets. No toys. That's what Billy and Bella told me," thought Teddy with a sigh.
"Hello, Teddy!" a voice called.
It was Barry Bear, one of Teddy's best friends.
Teddy was very pleased to see him.

He waved and smiled at Barry.

"You'll see Barry at playtime," said Daddy Bear. "He's older than you Teddy, so he won't be in your class."

Teddy didn't like the sound of that.

"Teddy Bear!" came a voice. "Lovely to see you!" It was Teacher Bear. "Hang your coat on this peg, the one with the picture of an engine. Do you like engines?" Teddy nodded.

"Then I want you to help Barbara feed the goldfish," Teacher Bear went on.

Barbara Bear smiled at Teddy.

"I'll show you what to do, Teddy," she said.

Then Teddy sat at the table next to Honey Bear, while the drawing things were being given out. Barry Bear's mummy was there too, sorting out lids from jam pots and coffee jars.

Soon Teddy was drawing round the lids, making a picture of a lovely bunch of balloons!

"I'm going to draw lots of trees!" said Tiny Bear. "Will you help me please, Teddy?"

And when all the lunch-boxes were opened, nobody minded about not having any sweets. "Teacher Bear says fruit and crisps are better for your teeth," explained Barry Bear.

There was time for games in the playground.
Teddy loved climbing up the slide into a little
hut, crawling through and then sliding down
the other side.

Later on, he filled lots of paper cups with sand
from the sand tray, ready to weigh them on
the classroom scales.
And what a lovely smell there was, coming
from the school kitchen!

"Dinner time!" called Teacher Bear, ringing a little bell.

"Cheese and tomato pizza!" cried Teddy, sniffing hungrily. And he ate every bit, followed by some cool, strawberry jelly.

After dinner, Teddy's class went into the playroom. What toys there were! Puzzles and bricks, tricycles, push-along toys, trains . . . There was no need to bring toys from home!

Teddy and his friends had just finished a big jigsaw when Teacher Bear clapped her hands. "Storytime!" she cried. "Put away the toys, then we'll go back to the classroom."

Teacher Bear had a lovely, big story-book with lots of pictures for everyone to see. Then they sang songs and nursery rhymes, clapping their hands in time to the music.

And when Teacher Bear said it was time to go home, Teddy thought about all the things he had done. He remembered the lovely dinner and the fun he'd had with all his new friends.

177

"Why did you say that you didn't like school?"
he asked Billy on the way home.
"We said there were no sweets!" grinned Billy.
"And that's true!"

"We said we couldn't bring toys!" said Bella. "But we never said we didn't LIKE school!" And they ran off laughing. Teddy laughed too. He knew he would see them at school the next day.

Lady and Rover

Every day, Rover, the sheep-dog at Buttercup Farm, waited at the gate to see his friend, Lady. She was a splendid white poodle, with a smart collar and a ribbon bow tied on top of her head. Lady lived in a big white house at the end of the lane.

As soon as Rover saw Lady, his tail began to wag and he gave a friendly bark. 'Woof! Hello, Lady! I have been waiting for you!' Lady was always pleased to see Rover.

Sooner or later, there always came a sharp voice. 'Lady! Come here! You will get your feet wet!' Or – 'Just look at your lovely, woolly coat! It is COVERED in mud!'

Really, Lady only had a few splashes of mud. But Miss Fox, the lady she lived with, was always fussing about her dog. She did not like Lady getting in a mess!

Rover was looking forward to seeing Lady in the big parade at the Dog Show! With her ribbons and pretty bows, he was sure she would win first prize!

And Rover? He was going to be in the
Sheep-Dog Competition, showing everyone
how well he could round up sheep and put
them safely into the pen.

Tim, the shepherd, had trained Rover since
he was a puppy. He only had to use his
whistle and Rover knew what to do. It was
a special whistle that only dogs can hear.

As the day of the Dog Show got nearer, the more Lady was brushed and groomed and fussed over. 'You are sure to win first prize!' smiled Miss Fox. 'I shall be SO proud of you!'

Even on the day of the Dog Show, Miss Fox
kept brushing Lady's coat and polishing her
little claws. Lady did not like it very much.
She wanted to see her friend, Rover.

Soon it was time for Lady and Miss Fox to
parade in the show ring. 'Hold your head
up high, Lady!' said Miss Fox. 'Let the
judges see what a pretty dog you are!'

People who were watching began to clap.
'What a lovely dog!' said one lady to her
friend. 'I do hope the judges choose her.
She deserves to win the prize!'

And in another field, Rover was also doing well! He had rounded up a flock of sheep and got them all together. Now all he had to do was to get them into the pen.

Tim blew his whistle as a signal for Rover. But, in the show ring, Lady heard it too! She knew that sound very well! It was Tim whistling for Rover!

Miss Fox felt Lady pulling at her lead.
'Stop, Lady!' she cried. 'Be a good girl!'
Tim blew his whistle again. This time, Lady
gave a loud bark. She tugged at her lead
more strongly.

Then Lady stood on her back legs and pawed at the air. That was the sound of Rover's whistle! Miss Fox could not hear it, but Lady could! She knew that her friend was somewhere near.

'Stop, Lady!' cried poor Miss Fox. But it was no good. Lady pulled so hard at her lead, she pulled Miss Fox over, right into the mud! 'Oh, no!' she moaned. 'My lovely, new suit!'

But that was not all. Lady was running into the
next field, mud and clumps of grass flying
everywhere! She looked around for Rover, but
all she could see was a whole lot of sheep!

Lady ran around the sheep, first one way, and then the other, just as she had watched Rover doing. Before long, she had got all the sheep into a tidy little group.

'Oh, no!' cried Miss Fox again, so loudly that everyone could hear. 'Just look at my beautiful poodle, Lady! She is dirty, she is muddy, she is untidy, she – she ...'

'She has just rounded up all those sheep and got them safely into the pen!' said Tim with a grin. 'Without anyone training her, too! What a clever dog she is!'

'Winner of the beginner class in the Sheep-Dog
Competition!' boomed the voice of a judge.
'But I do not have the name of this poodle!
What is she called? Who does she belong to?'

'She belongs to me!' cried Miss Fox. Now, she sounded very proud indeed! 'And her name is Lady!'
Then everyone began clapping and cheering all over again.

Tim led Rover across to see Lady. The two friends rubbed noses and wagged their tails. They were both so pleased to win a prize! As for Tim and Miss Fox, they started talking.

Lady is still a splendid white poodle, with pretty ribbons and a bow on top of her head. And Rover is still a hard-working sheep-dog with mud on his paws.

But Miss Fox does not bother so much about Lady getting her feet wet. Lady and Rover are together nearly all the time. And so are Tim and Miss Fox!

Teddy
and Baby Bear

It was the day of the Teddy Bears' Picnic! Everyone in Bear Village had been busy. The picnic food was ready and the playing fields were marked out ready for the games later on. Teddy was helping Barry Bear to put paper cups and plates on a long, wooden table. Soon everyone would be ready for a tasty picnic feast.

"You're such a help, Teddy," smiled Teacher Bear, as she carried bottles of milk and fruit squash to the table. "Could you do a very special job for me? It would be a great help."

"What sort of job?" asked Teddy. "Well," said Teacher Bear, "my sister is coming to help at the picnic, and we need someone sensible to look after her little bear, Baby Boo."

"There they are," cried Teacher Bear, before Teddy could answer. "Hello, Bonny. Hello, Baby Boo."

Teddy Bear blinked. He had never seen a bear who looked quite as sweet as Baby Boo!

"Now, Baby Boo," Teacher went on, "you play with Teddy while Mummy helps with the picnic. You will make sure she doesn't get dirty, won't you Teddy?" Teddy nodded his head.

"Hey, Teddy!" came the voice of Baker Bear.
"Come and help blow up a few balloons."
"Hear that, Baby Boo?" grinned Teddy. "You
won't get dirty if you watch me blowing up
balloons."

But Baby Boo did not seem very interested in balloons. What she wanted was to see what was inside a big flower pot!

"No, Baby Boo!" cried Teddy Bear.

"Don't get yourself dirty!"

Poor Teddy! He didn't see the tin of whitewash Painter Bear had brought to mark out a game of hopscotch on the grass. How Baby Boo laughed to see Teddy covered with big white blobs!

"Here's a cloth," cried Baker Bear.
But Teddy could not stop! Baby Boo was already toddling off towards a big basket of fat, juicy strawberries..."
"Don't get dirty!" cried Teddy.

SPLOSH! Teddy shut his eyes tight.
Then he opened them again. He let out a
deep breath. Baby Boo was not at all dirty.
HE was covered in bright red splodges of
strawberries!

Baby Boo laughed so much that Billy and Bella Bear came over to see what the joke was. Then they saw Teddy.

"What happened?" grinned Billy. He and Bella thought Teddy looked so funny!

"It's Baby Boo!" growled Teddy. "I'm supposed to make sure that she doesn't get dirty! Teacher Bear is counting on me!"

"Well, take her to the swings," Bella suggested. "She won't get dirty there."

That sounded a good idea to Teddy. Then Baby Boo decided she wanted a drink at the water fountain. "Mind that puddle!" warned Teddy Bear. "Don't get yourself dirty!"

SPLASH! Baby Boo didn't step into the puddle, but Teddy Bear did! Baby Boo looked down at her clean paws and her clean clothes. Then she looked at Teddy, and started laughing again.

Baby Boo didn't stop to see how angry Teddy was. She had just seen a big tub of sawdust that Mummy Bear had brought for the lucky dip. It was just inside a big tent, and Baby Boo headed straight for it.

"Baby Boo!" Teddy Bear shouted. "Come here!" He dashed into the tent after her. The next thing he knew, there was a shower of sawdust, grass and earth flying about. The tent fell down around him.

He could hear voices outside.

"What's happened to the tent?"

"Didn't Teddy Bear go inside?"

"Teddy? But I asked him to look after Baby Boo! He was supposed to see she didn't get dirty!" said Teacher.

"Baby Boo?" said Baker Bear. "She walked straight past the tent." There was silence. Slowly, very slowly, and with bears pulling and pushing and prodding him, Teddy Bear crawled out.

Nobody knew what to say.

"Teddy!" gasped Mummy Bear at last. "What HAVE you been doing?"

"I've been looking after Baby Boo," Teddy protested, "making sure she didn't get dirty!"

"My little Baby Boo?" said her mummy. "Just look at her! She's kept herself BEAUTIFULLY clean!"

"Yes, but..." began poor Teddy.

"YOU'RE covered with sawdust and muddy splashes!" said Teacher.

"And there are sticky strawberries on your fur!" said Baby Boo's mummy.
"To say nothing of all that white-wash!" sighed Mummy Bear. "Oh, Teddy! On the day of the Teddy Bears' Picnic, too!"

"Wait a minute," said Baker Bear. "Teddy DID look after Baby."

"And he made sure she didn't get dirty," added Barry Bear.

"And there's no harm done," said Daddy Bear.

"Only a bit of cleaning-up to do," said Mummy, beginning to smile. "Come along Teddy."

So Teddy was soon enjoying the picnic with his friends. And Baby Boo? Well, she got VERY dirty!

Timmy the Tortoise

Timmy the Tortoise had been a part of the family for as long as Joe could remember. Timmy was much older than Chips, the dog. He was even older than Joe himself.

'Your Grandad brought Timmy home when I was a boy!' Joe's dad often said. 'And he is still going strong!'

But, like all tortoises, Timmy was also very slow! While Joe and Chips raced up and down the garden, Timmy just sat on the grass, peeping out of his shell.

'Old slow-coach!' barked Chips. 'Even Horace the hamster is faster than you! Half the time Joe cannot even see you moving about in your dull shell!'

But Timmy did not mind being slow. He liked to stop and watch butterflies flying about, or a hedgehog rolling into a prickly ball, then unrolling again.

Then, one day, Joe called, 'Here, boy!'
'Mind out, Timmy!' barked Chips.
'Not you, Chips!' laughed Joe. 'It's Timmy
that I want.'

'I want to see where you are, Timmy!' said
Joe. 'So I am putting this white paint on
your shell, then everyone can find you! Isn't
that a great idea?'

Timmy was not sure that he liked wearing
white paint! But Joe looked pleased.
'Put that tortoise down, Joe!' said Mum.
'I want you to help me!'

'Grandma is coming to stay with us for a little while,' said Mum. 'She will be arriving soon!'
Joe liked Grandma!
'Coming!' he cried and ran down the path.

Chips ran after Joe and Timmy followed
Chips, slowly, as usual.
'Slow-coach!' Chips barked. 'Now we can
see just how slow you are!'

Joe and Chips ran inside, leaving Timmy in the garden. For once, he did wish he could run like Chips. After all, Chips was never left out of anything.

Timmy was still feeling sorry for himself when Chips came out again. This time, he was with a pretty little poodle dog.
'Fifi!' called a voice. 'Don't go too far!'

'Chips will look after Fifi!' said Joe. 'They're friends already!' But Grandma was looking at Timmy. 'That old tortoise!' she cried. 'He never changes!'

Timmy did not like the sound of that! Seeing Chips and Fifi playing together made him feel old, and very, very slow! As for Fifi, she was hardly ever still!

Fifi was always rushing around! One afternoon, she was even more fidgety than usual. 'Fifi!' cried Joe. 'Stop jumping in and out of my pool!'

But Fifi had not finished! She jumped up at
Joe's Dad, pawing at his leg and barking
all the time. Timmy was glad to stay in the
shade, out of the way!

'I think there is going to be a storm!'
cried Mum. 'It has been so hot today!
Bring your things inside, Joe, as quickly
as you can!'

Joe just had time to put on his shirt and shorts before the rain began.

'Get everything in the shed!' yelled Dad.

'That was a flash of lightning just now!'

As they rushed indoors, there came a clap of thunder. Chips growled. Fifi started barking. Before anyone could stop her, she ran out into the storm!

'No wonder she's been so jumpy!' said Dad. 'She knew the storm was on its way!' 'Fifi!' cried Grandma. 'Come back, Fifi! Don't be frightened!'

They stood at the door, calling Fifi's name. The storm made everywhere very dark. But Joe could just see a splash of white moving along very slowly...

'That's Timmy!' he cried. 'But he NEVER stays out in a thunderstorm like that!' Then Joe had an idea. 'Maybe we ought to go and see why, Grandma!'

Grandma fetched her umbrella and they
went outside. The thunder and lightning
had stopped, but it was still raining.
'Look!' cried Joe. 'There's Timmy!'

And as Timmy made his way slowly all the way to the end of the garden, Grandma and Joe followed. 'Fifi!' cried Grandma. 'Oh, Fifi! Where are you?'

Then, as Timmy got to the shed, they heard
a tiny, little whimper. 'Fifi!' cried Grandma
joyfully. 'Did the storm frighten you?'
She held out her arms and Fifi jumped up.